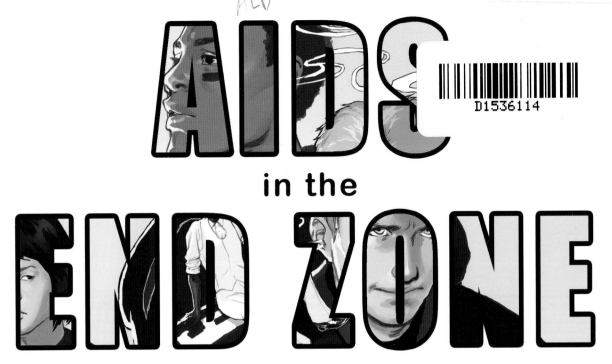

AIDS

in the

END ZONE

Edited by Kendra S. Albright and Karen W. Gavigan

Illustrated by Sarah J. Petrulis

The University of South Carolina Press

Characters

 Marcus Johnson, 17. and his parents have just moved from Texas to South Carolina. Beginning his senior year at the Marina High School is at first daunting, but he quickly finds success and popularity through his incredible football talent.

 Brad Timmerman, 17, lives with his rich, self-absorbed grandmother. He has the run of the house with no curfew and gets anything he wants. Popularity came easy to him as the star quarterback, until the arrival of Marcus Johnson.

 Sean Wongsawat, 17, is Brad's best friend and hangs out with the popular crowd. A star wide receiver, Sean looks like a shoe-in for a full college football scholarship, thanks to his best friend's support on the field. His family have struggled to make ends meet since they came to the U.S. from Thailand when Sean was three.

 Seth Henderson, 18, is a man of mystery. He works many hours to support his mother and sister. Although a loner, Seth always knows what's going on around the school.

 Maria Cruz, 17, is a party girl, beautiful, stylish, and popular, especially with the boys. Her parents divorced when she was a baby, and she lives with her mother and grandmother who work full time.

 Id, as the name suggests, is an ageless creature who always encourages the immediate gratification of all desires. Some consider Id to be the devil on your shoulder.

MARCUS JOHNSON:

NEW KID AT MARINA HIGH.

FIRST DAY OF SCHOOL.

I WISH I WAS AT MY OLD SCHOOL...

EEEEEEEK!!!

?

IT'S--

--BRAD TIMMERMAN

3

HEY DUDE!

SO THERE'S THIS CONCERT TONIGHT AND I THOUGHT YOU AND I SHOULD....UH...

UH...
...DUDE...?

I'M GOING CRAZY!!!!

I NEED TO GET MY SPOT BACK!!

DID YOU KNOW?
HIV IS A VIRUS THAT WEAKENS YOUR IMMUNE SYSTEM BY DESTROYING IMPORTANT CELLS THAT FIGHT DISEASE AND INFECTION.
THERE IS NO CURE FOR HIV, BUT IT IS TREATABLE.

AIDS IS THE DISEASE YOU GET WHEN HIV DESTROYS YOUR BODY'S IMMUNE SYSTEM.

HEY, MARIA!

WHAT.

C'MERE I NEED TO TALK TO YOU.

IF YOU KNOW WHAT'S GOOD FOR YOU, YOU'RE GOING TO SLEEP WITH MARCUS.

WHEN YOUR IMMUNE SYSTEM FAILS, YOU CAN GET SICK AND DIE.

HIV CAN BE TRANSMITTED THROUGH SEXUAL CONTACT WITH MEN OR WOMEN, WHETHER HOMOSEXUAL OR HETEROSEXUAL.

WHAT?? I'LL GET IN TROUBLE!

OH YEAH? DO YOU REALLY WANT THE WHOLE SCHOOL TO FIND OUT YOU HAVE HIV?

14

CLACK!

ROLL

ROLL

ROLL

THE NEXT DAY AT SCHOOL.

DID YOU KNOW?

THERE IS NO CURE FOR HIV, BUT ANTIRETROVIRAL MEDICATIONS ARE EFFECTIVE IN FIGHTING THE VIRUS.

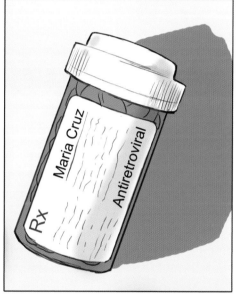

Rx   Maria Cruz   Antiretroviral

EXCUSE ME, MARIA. YOU DROPPED THIS...

UM... OH..THANKS, SETH...

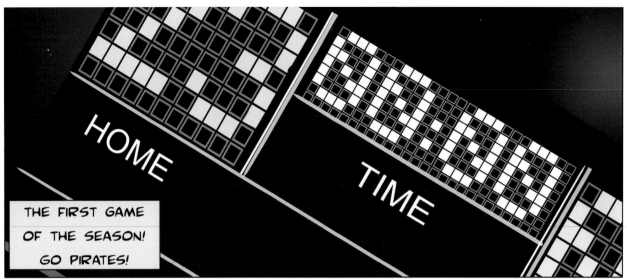

THE FIRST GAME OF THE SEASON! GO PIRATES!

TOUCHDOWN FOR MARCUS JOHNSON!
AND THAT'S A WIN FOR THE MARINA HIGH SCHOOL PIRATES!!

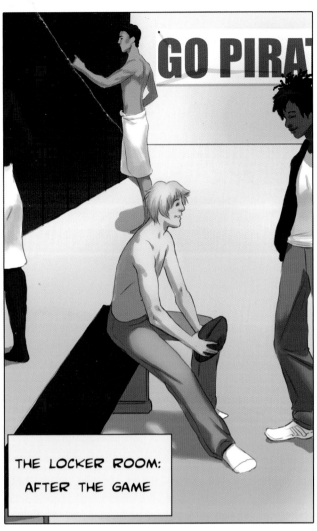

THE LOCKER ROOM:
AFTER THE GAME

HEY.

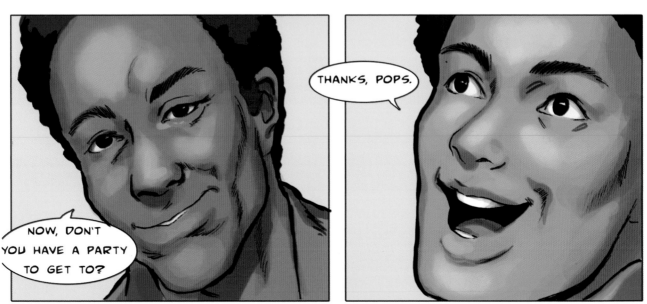

20

A PARTY RAGES AT THE TIMMERMAN MANSION.

HEEY JOHNSON.

LEMME INTRODUCE YOU TO MARIA.

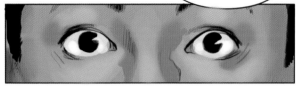

HI, MARCUS. YOU WERE AWESOME TONIGHT.

HAVE A BEER AND GET ACQUAINTED.

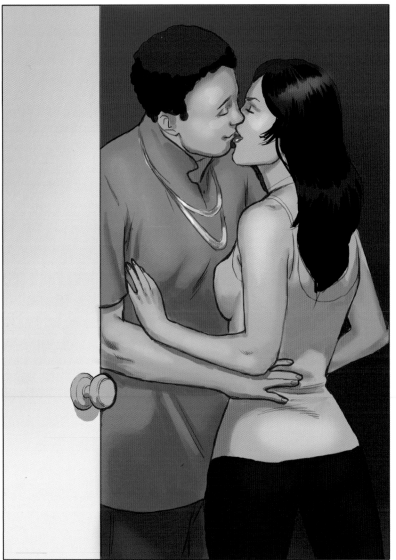

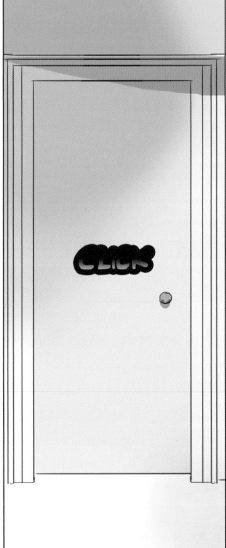

20 MINUTES LATER...

23

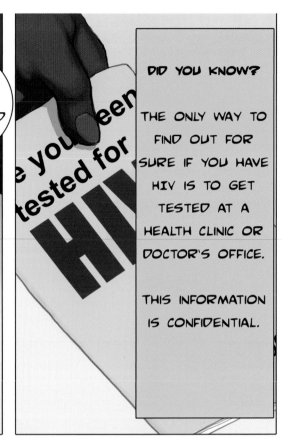

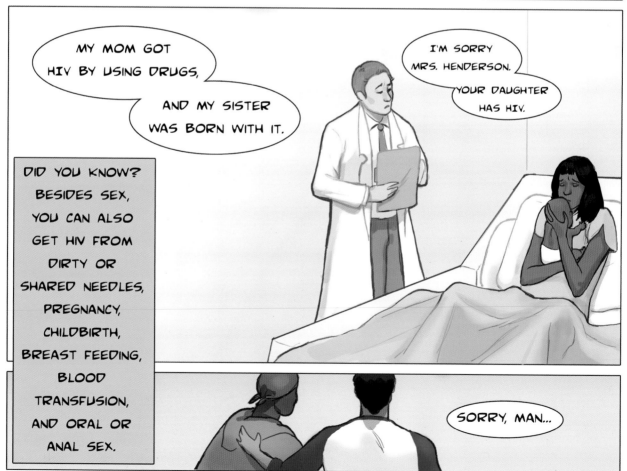

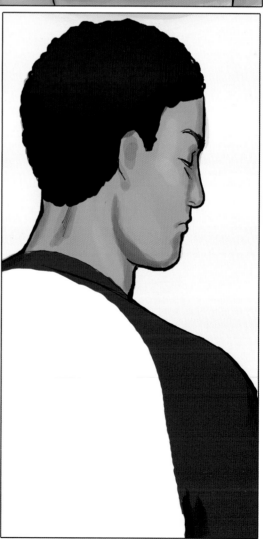

31

SENTENCING DAY...

THESE ARE VERY SERIOUS CRIMES! DO YOU HAVE ANYTHING TO SAY FOR YOURSELVES?

...NAH.

I...I JUST WISH IT HAD NEVER HAPPENED. AND TO MARCUS... I'M SO SORRY.

WHAT A LIAR! TRY TO GET HER SENTENCE INCREASED!

THIS WAY, MR. TIMMERMAN.

HMPH.

POOF!

MAN, I'M TIRED OF LISTENING TO YOU!

YOUR HONOR, I HAVE SOMETHING I WANT TO SAY.

MARIA...MARIA DOESN'T DESERVE JAIL TIME.

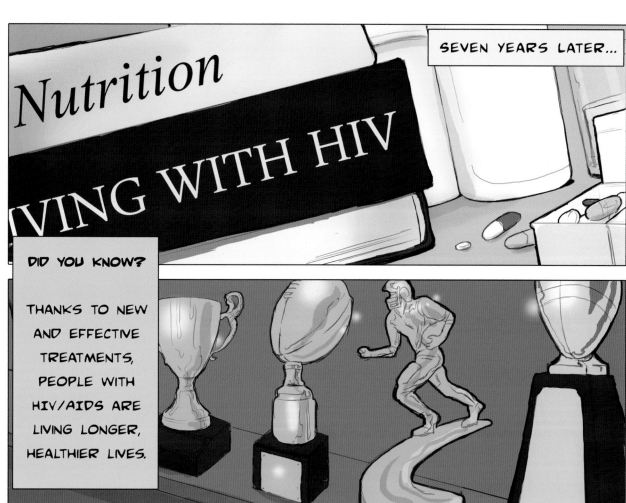

Did You Know?

What is HIV?

The Human Immunodeficiency Virus (HIV) prevents the human immune system from getting rid of most of the viruses in your body that can make you sick. People with HIV can live long and healthy lives, if they have access to treatment.

Symptoms of HIV may include weight loss, frequent fevers and sweats, lack of energy, swollen lymph glands, persistent skin rashes, severe herpes infections (mouth, genital, or anal sores), and short term memory loss. PLEASE NOTE: These can be symptoms of other illnesses. The ONLY way to know for sure if you have HIV is to get tested!

What is AIDS?

Aquired Immunodeficiency Syndrome (AIDS) is the final stage of the HIV infection. People at this stage of the HIV disease have badly damaged immune systems, which puts them at risk for opportunistic infections (for example, certain cancers) that can lead to severe illness and death.

You CAN get HIV/AIDS through:

Sexual contact with women or men, homosexual or heterosexual, including oral and anal sex

Drug use with dirty or shared needles

Pregnancy and birth (a child can be infected in utero or during birth if their mother is already HIV positive)

Breastfeeding

Blood transfusion

Through physical contact with someone with HIV who is bleeding

You can NOT get HIV/AIDS through:

Kissing someone who has HIV

Swimming in a pool with someone who has HIV

Toilet Seats

Hugging someone with HIV

Being in the same room with someone who has HIV

Inheriting it from a parent (although it can be passed through breastfeeding or pregnancy)

Tears, sweat, or saliva

Drinking fountains

Insect bites

Donating blood

Prevention:

You can prevent HIV through abstinence, using condoms, not sharing or using needles.

Condoms, when used correctly and ever time, are very useful in preventing HIV and other sexually transmitted infections (STIs).

It is not possible to know if someone has HIV/AIDS just by looking at them.

Alcohol and drugs can lead you to make bad choices about sex.

HIV tests and their results are confidential and will be shared ONLY with people authorized to see your medical records.

Glossary

Abstain/abstinence—avoiding certain behaviors, including sex.

AIDS—Acquired immune deficiency syndrome - the disease you get when your immune system fails. It is not genetic and can include the development of certain infections and/or cancers.

Antiretroviral drugs—Antiretroviral drugs are medications for the treatment of infections by retroviruses, primarily HIV.

HIV—human immunodeficiency virus - the virus that can lead to acquired immune deficiency syndromem, or AIDS. HIV damages a person's body by destroying specific blood cells, called CD4+ T cells, which are crucial to helping the body fight diseases (CDC, 2006).

Blood transfusion—transfer of blood, or blood production, from one person to another.

Condom—a thin rubber sheath worn on a man's penis during sexual intercourse that prevents pregnancy and protects against infection.

Immune system—the integrated body system of organs, cells, and tissues that protects the body against disease.

Infection—an organism that makes people sick. It is often contagious.

Sexually transmitted infections (STIs)—infections that are generally transmitted through sexual contact. Organisms that carse sexually transmitted infections may pass from person to person in blood, semen, or vaginal and other bodily fluids.

Virus—a microorganism that cannot grow or reproduce apart from another living cell.

For More Information

AIDS.gov. (n.d.). HIV/AIDS Basics. Washington, DC: Department of Health and Human Services. http://aids.gov/hiv-aids-basics

Avert. (2012). AIDS. West Sussex, UK: Avert International. http://www.avert.org/aids.htm

Avert. (2012). HIV. West Sussex, UK: Avert International. http://www.avert.org/hiv.htm

Centers for Disease Control (CDC). (2013). HIV/AIDS. Atlanta, GA: Department of Health and Human Services. http://www.cdc.gov/hiv

Mayo clinic. (2013). HIV/AIDS. Rochester, MN: Mayo Foundation for Medical Education and Research. http://www.mayclinic.com/health/hiv-aids/DS00005

Bethesda, MD: U.S. National Library of Medicine, National Institutes of Health. http://nlm.nih.gov/medlineplus/hivaids.html

TeensHealth. (2013). HIV and AIDS. Wilmington, DE: The Nemours Foundation. http://kidshealth.org/teen/sexual_health/stds/std_hiv.html

World Health Organization. (2013). HIV/AIDS. http://www.who.int/hiv/en

Webliography

AIDS Alliance for Children, Youth, &Families. http://www.aids-alliance.org

AIDS Healthcare Foundation. http://www.aidshealth.org

AIDSmeds. http://aidsmeds.com

American Public Health Association. http://www/apha.org/membergroups/sections/aphasections/hiv

American Sexual Health Association. http://www.ashastd.org/std-sti/hiv-aids.html

The Black AIDS Institute. http://www.blackaids.org

The Body. http://www.thebody.com/index/hotlines/other.html

HIV Insite. http://hivinsite.ucsf.edu

Latino Commission on AIDS. http://www.latinoaids.org

The Well Project. http://www.thewellproject.org/en_US

Acknowledgments

The editors would like to thank and recognize the authorship of this story by the young men at the South Carolina Department of Juvenile Justice (SCDJJ) in Columbia, SC. We would also like to thank the administration, faculty and staff at the SCDJJ for their ongoing support of this project.

Thanks also to Samantha Hastings, Director of the University of South Carolina School of Library and Information Science, and Charles Bierbauer, Dean of the College of Mass Communication and Information Studies for their support.

Funding for this project was recieved through a Carnegie Foundation Community Initative Grant though the University of South Carolina and the Association for Library and Information Science Education.

Published by the University of South Carolina Press
Columbia, South Carolina 29208

www.sc.edu/uscpress

Manufactured in the United States of America

Kim Shealy Jeffcoat, Series Editor

Contributors

Kendra Albright is an associate professor in the School of Library and Information Science at the University of South Carolina. Her research has focused on the role of information and communication in the prevention of HIV/AIDS and the ways in which people feel about different kinds of messages across different cultures.

Karen Gavigan is an assistant professor in the School of Library and Information Science at the University of South Carolina. She and Mindy Tomasevich are co-authors of Connecting Comics to Curriculum: Strategies for Grades 6-12 (Libraries Unlimited, 2011), and the Connecting Comics to Curriculum column in Library Media Connection.

Sarah Joy Petrulis studied illustration and painting at the University of South Carolina, The International School of Drawing, Painting, and Sculpture in Montecastello Italy, and the School of Visual Arts in Manhattan, NY. She believes strongly in the introspective and therapeutic benefits of creating stories and characters for people of all age groups.

The young men at the South Carolina Department of Juvenile Justice have done a great service to their peers and the state of South Carolina by authoring this book. Through collaborative input, they developed the concepts for the characters and brought them to life in a vivid story that aims not only to entertain but to educate young people about HIV/AIDS and help keep them safe.